CASTLE ON THE CLIFF

ZANDER BINGHAM

GREEN RHINO
MEDIA

www.greenrhinomedia.com

First Printing: December 2020

Green Rhino Media LLC
228 Park Ave S #15958
New York, NY 10003-1502
United States of America

www.jackjonesclub.com

ISBN 978-1-949247-21-3 *(Paperback - US)*

ISBN 978-1-949247-25-1 *(Paperback - UK/AU)*
ISBN 978-1-949247-22-0 *(eBook - US)*
ISBN 978-1-949247-26-8 *(eBook - UK/AU)*

Library of Congress Control Number: 2020922489

DEDICATION

To my wonderful and noble son, Xavier.
May you always conquer every quest in
life—big and small, of your own making, or
those the world throws your way—with a
kind heart, and a determined spirit.

CONTENTS

CHAPTER ONE

"Wow, this place in incredible!" Jack's jaw dropped in awe as he sprang from the back seat of his parents' car.

Emma and Albert quickly followed and stood alongside Jack as they stared upward. Looming over them, and perched proudly atop a cliff, the gray stone fortress was certainly an impressive sight. The castle was crowned with red peaks and adorned with bright flags and banners.

"It sure is something special," Mrs. Jones observed, her shoes crunching on the gravel driveway as she strolled over to join them.

"What's the big deal, it's not *that* different from our house, is it?" Mr. Jones chuckled as he began unloading the luggage.

"Dad!" Emma giggled as she broke into a playful twirl. "This place is ginormous. It's like five stories tall—and we don't have towers like *those* at home."

Mr. Jones laughed. "Well, yes, I guess there are a *few* differences."

A loud groan drew everyone's attention toward the front entrance as a heavy door opened. Two people began down the stairs and across the wooden bridge toward them.

"Hello there! Welcome to Elkmire Castle. You must be the Jones family." The woman had plump rosy cheeks; her black hair, sprinkled with a few white strands, was neatly fixed in a long braid that almost reached her waist.

"Yes indeed, that's us!" Mrs. Jones replied. "It's lovely to meet you. I'm Penelope, that's my husband Theodore, and these are our children Jack and Emma, and their friend, Albert."

"Such a pleasure to have you here. I'm Alice and this is my husband Oscar. Welcome to our humble home."

The children froze, seeming to all be thinking the same thing.

"Wait, you actually *own* this castle?" asked Jack as he fiddled with the zipper of his lucky jacket.

"Well, sometimes it feels like the castle owns *us*," Oscar joked, removing his brown tartan cap and scratching his forehead. "But, yes... it's ours alright, been passed down in Alice's family since it was built."

"So, does that make you a queen or a princess?" Emma asked excitedly, rocking back and forth on the tips of her toes.

Alice smiled warmly. "Alas no, my ancestors were noble families and knights, but not kings and queens."

"You own this castle *and* you're descended from knights? That's out-of-this-world cool!" Albert chimed in with an approving nod.

"Why, thank you, kind sir. I hadn't quite thought about it that way before, but I agree, it is pretty cool, as you say," Alice replied.

"And I suppose all the upkeep isn't that bad... a labor of love, really," Oscar added, his gray hair shining in the sunlight.

"And the view—I'm sure you never get tired of that, either." Mrs. Jones stared out over the cliff toward the deep blue ocean dotted with small islands in the distance.

A cool breeze blew in, carrying the smell of salty sea air and the sound of seagulls squawking as they flapped about in the sky.

"No, neither of us has ever taken that for granted. It's as special now as it was when I was little," Alice smiled fondly at Oscar and hugged his arm. "I was raised here with my younger brother and sister; they visit a few times a year. Oscar and I have two children of our own, but they are grown up now and moved to the city with their families. So, these days it's just us here," Alice explained.

"And of course, there's Wilbur, the caretaker," Oscar added. "He's been at Elkmire since Alice was a girl and has a house on the grounds. And every now and then we're lucky enough to have visitors such as yourselves. We have plenty of space!" Oscar waved his arm toward the sprawling castle behind him.

"Well, we certainly appreciate you letting us stay. Penny and I will be tied up with the conference for most of the long weekend, and we figure that exploring the castle will keep the kids entertained," said Mr. Jones.

"Absolutely, you're going to love it! I had so many adventures with my siblings growing up; we got into plenty of mischief inside the castle and in the surrounding woods as well. Oh my, we used to play princesses and knights and explorers... so many wonderful memories. Come on now, let me show you around," said Alice as she turned toward the stairs and welcomed them inside.

"Can I help you with your luggage?" Oscar asked.

"No thanks, we're used to traveling, so we pack light," Jack replied as he slung his backpack over his shoulder and began toward the castle.

The grand, stone entrance hall was wondrous. The vast rectangular room drew their eyes up to a soaring ceiling that was two-stories high and supported by heavy wooden beams.

In the middle of the room was a wide staircase that split halfway up, with each side heading toward opposite areas. A second-floor hallway was open to the entrance hall, broken only by stone support pillars and wooden railings.

Jack's eyes flashed with amazement as he looked around. Every inch of the wall space seemed to be covered with framed portraits, colorful tapestries, and medieval armor.

Alice chuckled as she caught Jack's eye. "Quite amazing, isn't it?"

"Yeah," Jack nodded. "I mean, all of this stuff is so awesome!"

"I'm glad you think so. There's many, many generations of my family represented on these walls." Alice pointed out a large portrait of her grandparents seated beside a fireplace, and one of her mother and father.

"Wow, are you related to *all* of these people?" Albert asked.

"Yes, everyone you see on these walls was once an owner of Elkmire. The castle has

stood for over nine hundred years, and many of the faces you see up here added to it or changed it during their time."

"Are you two up here somewhere?" asked Jack, squinting as he searched the faces.

"Not yet... our portrait is being painted now, it's a bit of a tradition. The artist has been working on it for a month or so and when it's finished, we'll add it to the collection. So long as we can find some empty wall space, that is," Alice giggled.

"And what are all of these? Family jewels?" Emma asked eagerly as she wandered toward a group of display cases near the middle of the room.

"Indeed! These treasures have been in our family for generations—some date all the way back to medieval times; kings and queens, and knights in shining armor," explained Oscar as the group huddled around the displays.

Jewelry made of gold and silver, much of it adorned with precious gems, filled one of the cases. Another contained a full suit of armor, complete with an iron sword and shield. A third case held scrolls and well-worn books from ages past.

"My parents actually had these displays built. They had ideas to turn the castle into a museum, but that never happened," Alice shrugged.

"Oh, something's missing from this one," said Albert, drawing everyone's attention to a mostly empty case with only a few trinkets around the sides. "The sign says *Sword of Dragon's Fire.*"

"Wow, that sounds neat!" Emma hurried over and placed her hands on the glass as she peered in, her breath forming a foggy cloud on the surface.

"Sword of Dragon's Fire?" Jack was wild with curiosity. "What's that?"

CHAPTER TWO

"We're fairly sure the Sword of Dragon's Fire existed," said Oscar. "A few historical experts have researched it along with the knights of the Order of the Dragon, and it was said to have belonged to Xavier the Dragon Heart. He was the founding member, and it was he who built this castle. His sword was one of the most sacred possessions of the order. They believed it had almost magical abilities to lead them to victory in battle."

"So, where is it now?" asked Jack.

"We don't know," Alice replied softly. "Lost or hidden or pillaged long, long ago. My parents were convinced that the sword, along with a whole trove of treasures the knights had accumulated, was hidden here in the castle somewhere but were never able to find them."

"Well, surely it didn't just vanish," said Emma, folding her arms across her chest.

"I agree," Oscar nodded, "but it's never been found here or elsewhere. We've visited many museums and private collections over the years and spoken with collectors and historians, most of whom knew about the sword, or at least the legend of it, but none had ever come across it."

"That's the real mystery," added Alice. "Everyone seems to agree that the sword existed, but no one knows its whereabouts."

"Whatever happened to the knights?" asked Albert.

"Tremendous question!" Alice replied with a big grin.

"She loves any chance to share everything she's learned about them," joked Oscar.

Alice chuckled, "Well, yes I do... it's quite a remarkable story, really. Xavier Wakefield was born in the year 1070 to Lord Kendrick and Lady Irvette Wakefield. Being the youngest of five children, he was not very likely to inherit his family's estate or title. He trained to become a knight and his skills and courage earned him a position in the king's guard. Through hard work and determination, Xavier rose to become commander, which meant that in battle he was responsible for leading the group."

"Wow, that must have been dangerous, being a knight back in medieval days," Albert mused.

"Most certainly. Many did not survive to old age," said Alice.

"So how did he get his own castle if he wasn't the king?" Jack was curious.

"Well," Alice continued, "the king's guard, under Xavier's lead, became well known as a most capable and loyal group of warriors. They would travel to the far ends of the kingdom, keeping the peace and carrying out the king's directives. King Stanford was known as a good king who was intelligent and fair, and the realm prospered under his rule."

Alice raised a finger and pursed her lips, "That didn't mean he wasn't without enemies though, and in 1102 an invading army from the neighboring kingdom made it past the outposts and began marching on King Stanford's castle, and the seat of the throne."

"No way!" Emma blurted. "Then what happened?"

Alice giggled, seeming to appreciate the children's enthusiasm. "The king assembled his army and they set out to repel the invaders. Of course, the king's guard rode with them as well."

"This is quite the tale," said Mr. Jones.

"It really is!" Albert agreed.

"See? I knew you'd like the story," Alice exclaimed, her cheeks looking even more rosy now. "Anyway, when the two armies met, there was a fierce battle. A small group of highly trained soldiers from the invaders managed to slip past the guards and reached the king's tent in the middle of the night. They say that Xavier sensed danger even as he slept, and he awoke to investigate. He discovered fallen guards nearby and rushed to the king, who was defending himself against the invaders. Xavier fought valiantly alongside him. They were outnumbered— ten enemy soldiers and only the two of them—and the king was gravely injured."

"Oh no, did the king... die?" Jack gulped.

"Not that night, no," Alice shook her head. "Based on historical accounts, he came awfully close. The king had been wounded and he collapsed. No longer able to defend himself, he was set upon by one of the soldiers. Xavier had just finished battling another intruder, when he saw what was about to happen, and rushed to help. By the king's own recorded account, Xavier threw himself between the king and his attacker and with his sword, vanquished the enemy soldier."

"So, he was a hero?" asked Jack.

Alice nodded. "Yes indeed, due to his bravery and skill he was able to save the king. The doctors were able to mend his wounds and he recovered, but it was Xavier's courage that saved King Stanford that night. Once word of his heroics spread through the camp, it inspired and rallied the army, and the following day they were victorious. In recognition of his remarkable feat, the king bestowed a lordship of his own and he became known as Sir Xavier the Dragon Heart. He was also granted this land."

"Neat," Albert whispered.

"Sir Xavier continued to lead the knights of the king's guard," Alice went on, "who became the Order of the Dragon, and were renowned not only throughout the kingdom but far beyond, too. Their exploits created considerable wealth, which they used to build this castle and establish their order. The sword itself became a symbol of inspiration, of good's triumph over evil."

Mrs. Jones grinned. "Well, that's an extraordinary story, Alice. I see why you like to tell it—and why you're so proud of your ancestors."

"But if it was so special, how come the sword can't be found now?" Emma moaned.

"Yah, well that's the big question, ain't it." The group turned toward a gruff, unfamiliar voice.

"There you are, Wilbur," said Oscar as he introduced the Jones family to the castle's caretaker. "Alice was just telling our guests all about the history of Elkmire."

Wilbur rolled up the sleeves of his faded blue and brown checkered shirt and stared up toward one of the imposing stone walls. Everyone else seemed to follow his gaze.

"What are you looking at, Wilbur?" Emma asked.

"Well, I was just thinking about my theory on where the sword is..." he answered, scratching his head.

Jack, Emma, and Albert gasped.

CHAPTER THREE

"What's *your* theory about where the sword is?" asked Jack as he looked eagerly at the caretaker.

"Yes, please tell us, Wilbur," said Emma, who seemed as intrigued as her brother.

"Well, ya see that writing up there?" Wilbur asked, pointing up toward the stone wall.

"*Where trees once proud hold knowledge bound, follow what is written to secrets hidden.*" Albert read out the words chiseled into the stone.

"What does it mean?" asked Jack.

"Well, that's what everyone's been tryin' to figure out," Oscar smirked. "There are a few phrases like this scattered 'round the castle grounds. Let me think... there's this one, it seems to suggest the library—trees, knowledge, paper."

"Yeah, that makes sense," Jack agreed as he ran a hand through his blond hair.

"We've looked all around the library though, and couldn't find anything," said Alice.

Wilbur cleared his throat. "There's another clue that seems to reference the dungeons. I don't recall the exact words, but it's written on the fountain in the courtyard. We've searched the old dungeons and couldn't find anything there either. I reckon there's got to be a secret passage that hasn't been found yet. There are a few that we know of, quite possible there's more."

"Dungeons and secret passages? No way!" Emma exclaimed.

"Oh yes, the dungeons are quite a spooky place really, of course we don't use them anymore... unless someone is really naughty that is, so best behave yourselves," Oscar grinned.

"You hear that, kids? Better be good or you might be locked up," joked Mr. Jones.

"Dad, that's not funny!" Emma grumbled, furrowing her brow.

"And as for secret passages, there are three. One is... or, maybe I shouldn't say, perhaps you can see if you can find them while you're here?" Alice offered, rubbing her hands together.

"Finding the secret passages does sound cool, but I want to find that sword!" said Jack.

"How amazing would that be?" Emma's face lit up with excitement. "You know, we've found hidden treasure before."

"Really?" Alice replied curiously.

"It's true, these kids have quite the history of solving mysteries—like finding hidden pirate treasure and lost ancient relics in the jungle!" Mr. Jones grinned.

"Well, in that case, please feel free to search anywhere and everywhere. If we can help, just ask," said Alice.

"Wow, this is going to be so much fun!" Emma clapped her hands and jumped up and down, her hair bouncing wildly.

"I'd suggest you start with the clue riddles." Alice winked at Jack. "I reckon one of them will be the right one, just I'm not sure which. For all we know there may be others—there are over one hundred rooms in the castle, most of them we never even enter."

"Only if you're sure. Free rein in a castle like this is a pretty big offer," cautioned Mrs. Jones, "but if you mean it, that certainly will keep these adventurers highly entertained while Teddy and I are working this weekend. We're the hosts you see, so we'll be at the conference hall most of the day tomorrow and Sunday."

Alice waved her hands dismissively and shook her head. "Oh, it's fine, this castle has been standing for hundreds of years; it's withstood invasions, housed brave and chivalrous knights, and hosted kings and queens, so I don't think this precious group of fine and very polite children here, can hurt it."

A cheeky grin crept across Jack's face. "Thank you, Alice. We'll do our best not to let you down."

Albert twiddled his thumbs. "While we're on the subject of clues, why do you think they would openly leave them around the castle? I mean, if they wanted to keep things a secret and all?"

"Good question, young lad," Wilbur replied with a nod as he patted Albert on the shoulder. "After Sir Xavier built this castle, the order of knights continued to grow.

Eventually they had several castles around the kingdom and members from the order would travel from one castle to another."

"Okay..." said Jack.

"So, I reckon that they placed the clues in such a way that only another member of the order would know its meaning, or which was the right one to follow, so they could locate the secret chamber if they needed to. That's my theory on it, anyway. Hidden in plain sight," chuckled Wilbur.

"Interesting idea for sure," said Jack, as he looked at the words once more.

"Alice, can you tell me about that crest up there?" Albert pointed toward a tapestry hanging proudly in the middle of the wall opposite the entrance. It depicted a shield with an arrangement of stars on the front and winged dragons on either side.

"That is the Order of the Dragon's crest, which has been the symbol of the family since Sir Xavier's day. The blue represents truth and loyalty, and the silver means peace and sincerity. Those stars dotted in the middle of the shield form the constellation Draco, meaning dragon, which symbolizes the strength and courage of the order.

"Cool! Hey, maybe we should get a family crest?" Jack said as he looked at his parents.

"Hmm... not a bad idea, Jack, my boy. We could look into that," Mr. Jones winked as he appeared to ponder the idea.

Alice giggled, "Indeed! For now, though, the afternoon is getting on and I'm sure you'll be feeling hungry soon. Let me show you to your rooms so you can get settled in and then we can eat in the formal dining room."

"Yes, please, lead the way!" Jack exclaimed, patting his stomach. He was always up for a good feed.

Wilbur said he had a few more tasks to complete on the castle grounds before sunset, Oscar headed to the kitchen to begin preparing dinner, and Alice led everyone up the grand staircase. They encountered even more portraits and relics, each breathing life and detail into the magnificent history of the castle.

"Here we are. This is your room for the weekend," said Alice as she walked through a doorway off the main hall. "My kids stayed in here when they were about your age and so did I when I was a child!"

The doorway opened into the middle of a sizeable room where large windows spanned the long wall with views across the ocean. Two sets of wooden bunk beds with blue checkered bed linen and blankets were set off to the right. An enormous work desk sat near the windows to the left, and a few crates of toys, most looking well-loved, were tidily arranged along the wall behind the desk.

"I call top bunk!" cried Jack as he started running across the room.

"I want the one near the window!" called Emma as she skipped toward it.

"Oh, wait, Albert, where do you want to be?" Jack paused and turned back to his friend.

"You know I don't like heights, so you can take the top one," Albert smiled as he removed his backpack and tossed it onto the lower bunk.

"Great, it all works out then!" Alice grinned. "I'm going to show your parents to their room next door. See you downstairs in the dining room in about an hour, okay?"

"Yup, sounds great!" Jack replied.

Emma and Albert smiled.

The children washed up for dinner, then explored a bit of the castle before searching for the main dining room. They found a massive library, two sitting rooms, and a large ballroom before stumbling across the right place.

Over a delicious dinner of braised beef short ribs, herb-roasted vegetables, and mashed potatoes with gravy, the children listened as Oscar, Alice, and Wilbur shared more stories of the castle, valiant battles fought by the knights, and the clues about the possible hiding place of the Sword of Dragon's Fire.

CHAPTER FOUR

Jack blinked his eyes open as daylight began creeping in around the curtains. After a satisfying stretch, he sat up and kicked off the covers before leaping down from his bunk. The thud on the wooden floor startled Albert, who was still tucked in tightly, and Emma grumbled from her bed.

"What's going on, Jack?" Emma croaked.

"Up and at 'em. Time to start exploring!" Jack replied. "We've got a long-lost sword to find. Come on you two, get up." Jack rustled through his backpack and grabbed some clean jeans and a blue and white striped sweater. Then he hurried to the windows and began to pull the curtains open, letting sunlight fill the room.

"It's so bright," Emma groaned, rolling over and pulling the blankets over her head.

Albert yawned as he rubbed his eyes, put on his glasses, and got out of bed. "I guess we should get started, we're only here for two more days!"

"Hey, Em, the early bird gets the worm, remember?" Jack encouraged.

"I don't want any worms. I just want a bit more sleep," she mumbled.

"Oh, come on, we'll get some breakfast and then get started. Something tells me this will be a fun mystery to solve. The sword is here, I can feel it," Jack replied, trying his best to coax Emma from her slumber.

Emma griped a bit more before sitting up and stretching her arms. "Okay, okay, you're right, Jack; it is going to be pretty fun exploring this place."

After getting themselves dressed and ready for the day, Jack, Emma, and Albert bounded along the hallway and down the stairs to the kitchen where Mr. and Mrs. Jones were eating breakfast at a round table with Alice and Oscar.

"Good morning, you three. How did you sleep?" Mrs. Jones asked.

"Great!" answered Jack, "We're so ready to find that missing sword."

"Well, some of us are more ready than others," Albert joked as he looked to Emma, who frowned back at him.

"Hey, sometimes I'm just not a morning person." Emma pushed up the sleeves of her lilac sweater and spooned some cut fruit into a bowl.

"Only *sometimes*, Emma?" joked Mrs. Jones.

The group sat down together and enjoyed a healthy breakfast of scrambled eggs, toast, and fruit salad before Mr. and Mrs. Jones said their goodbyes and headed off to the conference hall to prepare for their meetings.

Alice and Oscar set off to the village to collect some groceries they needed while Wilbur tended to his list of maintenance tasks around the grounds, leaving the children to explore.

"So, where should we begin?" asked Jack as they left the kitchen.

"Well, if we want to follow Wilbur's theory then I guess we need to search for all the clues first, figure out what they mean, and then work out which one we think will lead us to the sword. It's possible some of the coded clues are just decoys, you know, to make it harder to find," explained Albert.

"Yeah, that makes sense to me, too," Jack agreed.

"What was the first clue again, the one in the entrance hall that talks about knowledge? I say we write it down, and check out the library in case we can find something they might have overlooked, and then go search for the other clues if we need to."

"Sounds like a good plan," said Emma.

"Don't worry, I've got my trusty notebook in my pocket. I can write them down," Albert offered as they made their way back to the entrance hall and jotted down the clue:

Where trees once proud hold knowledge bound, follow what is written to secrets hidden.

Next, the trio headed to the library they'd accidentally stumbled across the night before.

The library was a huge square room, with half-a-dozen small windows and towering bookcases which lined most of the walls from the floor all the way to the high ceilings overhead. The air had a distinct woody, earthy smell to it and there were two wooden rolling ladders, one on either side of the room to allow access to the books stored on the upper levels. There were rows and rows of books, ranging from ancient and delicate-looking leather-bound tomes to newer, less worn options covering a vast array of topics and interests from gardening to medieval history.

A large sandstone cast of a flying dragon with soaring wings occupied a section of wall nestled between several rows of bookshelves.

On the rear wall, alongside a tapestry of the Order of the Dragon's crest, hung a medieval armor display that also contained three tarnished iron swords and two wooden spears with pointy metal tips.

An enormous bronze globe that towered over the children was perched atop a round, beige podium made of stone and sat in the middle of the library.

There were two leather sofas, several reading chairs with footrests, and a large glossy table with a half-finished puzzle surrounded by the remaining pieces.

"What do you suppose we're looking for?" Emma asked as her eyes searched the library.

"Good question, I really have no idea," Jack replied as he contemplated the task ahead of them.

"It's probably not one of *these* swords, that would be too easy," said Albert as he crossed the room and admired the old items.

"Case closed, we didn't just find one missing sword, we found three. They were hiding in plain sight all along," Jack joked as he joined Albert and examined the display.

"I don't think so..." Emma replied as she walked over to the puzzle. "Look, it's going to be a puppy with two kittens, aww, so *cute!*"

Albert laughed, "I'm sure it is, Em, but if we're going to find this missing sword, finishing the puzzle probably won't help."

"Maybe it's a magical ancient puzzle and once we put it together, the sword will appear... yeah, probably not," Emma scrunched her nose and giggled. "So, what else could it be, then? Maybe the globe? It could be a map that leads to something." Emma began circling the globe while staring up at it. Jack nodded and joined her.

"It's possible... look, the countries, the continents, the land shapes are all wrong," Jack observed as he ran his hand along the rough stone of the podium. "I wonder what these holes are for, hmm there's a few of them."

"This must have been made a long time ago, before the whole planet had been mapped, said Albert. "I remember Mr. Atlas in geography class telling us that different leaders and explorers had maps of some areas of the world, but it took a while for all the pieces to be put together in one place."

"Just like the puzzle!" Emma joked.

Albert smiled. "That's true. And, also like the puzzle, for a long time they thought the world was flat. We kind of just take it for granted sometimes that we know all we do today, and we can just search the internet for answers."

"Right!" Emma agreed.

"You just blew my mind!" added Jack.

"As for these holes, hmm..." Albert paused and squatted down for a closer look at the tall, narrow diamond shapes cut into the sides of the stone. "Can't really see much inside them. Could just be decoration, or maybe something to do with how it was built, or how the globe was mounted to the podium. Hard to tell without a flashlight."

Jack traced the outline of one of the holes and peered inside. "I've got one in my backpack, but I left it in our room."

"Yup, I packed one, too," Emma replied from across the room where she was pulling books from the shelves and returning them.

"I never leave home without it. Well, not often anyway. We should go back up there later and get them," said Albert.

"What are you doing, Emma?" asked Jack as he stood up.

Emma giggled. "Well, you know how sometimes in movies they pull a book out from the shelf and it opens up a secret doorway behind the bookcase?"

"Ha! Good thinking, Em," said Jack. "But we could be here for a while if we try that theory. There must be thousands of books in here."

"It's probably unlikely, but I figured it was worth a try," Emma shrugged.

"Who knows, it might turn out to be right, but maybe we should take a look at all the clues around the place before we go pulling all of these books down. Maybe it's not even in the library at all," Jack replied.

"Yes, I think it's best to focus on the clues. Let's go and see what else we can find," Albert suggested.

"Sounds good to me," Emma agreed.

CHAPTER FIVE

Remembering what Wilbur had said about another coded clue, Jack, Emma, and Albert made their way outside and headed for the fountain.

The sun was shining in the bright blue sky, but it was a chilly spring day and the air felt brisk. Jack was glad he brought along his lucky jacket, and Albert flicked up the collar of his green plaid shirt, so it covered his neck a little. Emma retied her purple scarf as they went in search of their next clue.

The huge square courtyard was surrounded by the walls of the castle where the sound of flowing water seemed to echo off them. Several arched passageways led off in every direction. Two flower gardens, and a white rattan table surrounded by matching chairs fixed with blue and white cushions, provided a bright contrast to the dark gray of the stone.

In the center of the courtyard was a magnificent circular fountain made of white marble speckled with black patterns. In the middle stood an enormous statue of a dragon, its wings extended as the water sprayed out beneath its claws, giving the impression that the dragon was soaring above the sea.

"Pretty cool dragon statue," Jack remarked.

"Look, here's the clue Wilbur was talking about," said Albert, pointing toward the letters coming into view as they drew nearer.

"Nice, Albert! Let's see, what does it say? *Round and round, deep underground, leads the way to secrets found.*"

Jack repeated the phrase a few times, hoping to make some sense of it as Albert scribbled it down in his notebook.

"Does that mean we need to go *under* the castle?" asked Emma.

"That's what it sounds like, but Wilbur said he'd looked around the dungeons and didn't find anything," Albert replied.

"Remember Alice said that doorway in the kitchen led down to the basement and dungeon area? I think we should grab our flashlights and go and look ourselves," said Jack.

Albert shrugged, "Best lead we've got, I guess."

Emma nodded, and the three children raced back inside the castle and made their way to the kitchen.

Jack flipped on the old light switch as the three descended, one after the other, into the dimly lit basement.

"Eww, it smells so damp and stale," Emma whined as the stairs squeaked and creaked beneath them until they reached the stone floor.

There were only a few working lightbulbs, but Jack could see that the space was wide and seemed to stretch off into the distance in either direction. Old boxes and crates were haphazardly stacked all around. Most of them were dusty and didn't appear to have been moved in a long time.

Jack flicked on his flashlight. "Well, let's go this way first and see what we find."

Emma and Albert followed, shining their lights around as they headed deeper underground.

Further along, they came across a few more staircases. They explored each one; several led to rooms back inside the castle, and a couple led to trap doors which opened to outside areas around the castle grounds. Some were stairs or corridors to nowhere— just dead ends where the castle had been changed over the many years since it was first built. There were also narrow passageways leading to underground rooms, some empty, others stacked floor to ceiling with boxes of items big and small from long ago. Candlesticks, pitchers, bowls, jugs, bottles, and bigger items like beds, tables and chairs cluttered the area. But no sword.

"This place needs a map," Jack grumbled. "Where could the dungeons be? This just seems like a huge basement."

"Don't lose heart, Jack!" said Albert. "If this were an easy discovery to make, someone else surely would have found it by now."

"Exactly!" Emma encouraged. "Chin up and let's keep looking!"

After turning a corner, they found a room off to one side with a wide staircase leading upward to a wooden double door.

"Hmm, another staircase leading *up*," said Jack as he and Emma made their way over and shone their lights upward. "There's daylight creeping in around the door, it must go to outside."

Albert followed and tried to squeeze in behind Jack and Emma in the tight space.

"Aaaaaahhhh!"

Jack and Emma turned around to see that Albert had disappeared.

"Albert!" shrieked Emma as she and Jack shone their flashlights in the direction of Albert's scream.

They saw another staircase opposite the one they'd just found, but this one led further underground. The pair raced down in search of their friend. Albert sat in a crumpled heap near the bottom of the stairs, wincing in pain.

"Oh no!" cried Jack, "Are you okay, buddy?"

Albert straightened his glasses as Emma retrieved his flashlight, which lay at the bottom of the stairs, lighting an arc across the floor.

"Yeah, might have a few bruises tomorrow, and I feel so silly not seeing that staircase there, but otherwise I think I'll be fine."

Emma squeezed Albert tightly and he winced again. "Oops, sorry!" said Emma, realizing her tight hug had added to Albert's discomfort.

"Here, let me help you up," Jack offered. "Maybe we quit this adventure—it's not worth any of us getting hurt like this."

"No way!" Albert scoffed, shaking his head at Jack, "I'll be okay, just need a minute."

Albert stood slowly, groaning a little as he dusted himself off.

"Well, we're definitely deep underground now," Jack said, patting his friend on the shoulder and thinking about the clue from the fountain.

"Yeah, but what about the round and round part?" asked Emma, handing Albert his flashlight.

"Let's see what we find. Looks like there is some light up ahead. I wonder where that's coming from?" said Albert.

"It doesn't make any sense, but I feel like I can hear and smell the ocean," said Emma.

"Yeah, I hear that too. Come on, let's check it out," Jack replied as he stepped forward, waving his flashlight ahead to make sure there were no obstacles in their path.

CHAPTER SIX

It didn't take long for the three children to reach the end of the passageway, where a rusty metal gate sat ajar.

"Seems like your stumble has led us straight to the dungeon, Albert!" cried Jack excitedly.

The gate was heavy and seemed wedged in place.

"I think it's stuck like this. Probably the rust. Can you two give me a hand?" asked Jack as he continued to push.

Even with the three of them shoving with all their strength, they only managed to shift the gap in the gate slightly.

"Ugh, I don't think it will budge any further. Maybe we can squeeze past it?" Jack wondered aloud as he stepped back and shone his flashlight at the opening.

"Yeah, I'm sure I can," said Emma as she made her way through the opening. "See? Piece of cake."

Albert went next, followed by Jack, and although it was tight, they were both able to pass through.

"I'd say this is definitely the dungeon," said Albert as he shone his flashlight to the side, illuminating the corroded metal bars across the stone alcoves.

"There's light coming in from those windows," said Jack, pointing at the small openings in the stone at the back of each cell.

The group stayed close as they searched the area. There were a dozen individual cells, each big enough to hold about as many prisoners if they were squished in. Cobwebs sparkled in the light as they found names, letters, and some tally marks etched into the stone walls, likely left by prisoners long ago. When they reached the end of the cell block, they still hadn't found any new clues to help them track down the sword.

"I guess Wilbur was right, there doesn't seem to be anything here, it's another dead-end."

"Bummer," Emma sighed. "Well, let's not spend any more time than we need to down here, it's kind of creepy."

"So, where to next, then?" Albert asked as he swept the area with his flashlight one final time.

Jack rubbed his chin. "Hmmm, didn't Alice mention that there was a clue in the ballroom somewhere? I say we find it—

maybe that's the missing link to solving the whereabouts of this mysterious sword!"

Emma and Albert agreed, and the trio headed out of the dungeons and back inside the castle, their eyes squinting as they adjusted to the light once more.

The ballroom was long and wide, with arched windows along both sides that were draped with embroidered navy and silver curtains. There was a raised stage area, and six enormous iron and crystal chandeliers hanging from the tall ceiling overhead.

Emma shrieked when she saw the clue. In the middle of the room, about halfway up the wall and carefully carved into a decorative wooden panel, were the words:

As the world turns toward the east, look yonder to our winged beast.

"Sheesh, what does *that* mean?" said Jack, sounding frustrated.

Emma and Albert both laughed.

"Well, it could be a few things. The planet does turn toward the east and they kind of have a lot of dragon things around here—it's the mark on their crest, remember?" Albert replied as he wrote the new clue down on his notepad.

"Yeah, practically every room we've been in has had some kind of dragon. And there were more outside, too. Hmm, this clue is a bit trickier," said Emma as she stepped to the middle of the room and did a pirouette on the shiny wooden floor.

Just then, Jack's stomach grumbled. "Hey, are you guys hungry?"

"Starving," said Albert.

"I could eat," added Emma.

"Ok, let's grab a bite and then we can keep looking around this afternoon," suggested Jack as they made their way to the kitchen.

CHAPTER SEVEN

After lunch, the trio found themselves back in the entrance hall, where they studied the first clue again.

"Okay, so last night at dinner Alice said the last clue she knows about is in the knight's cabinet—and that looks like the massive doorway she said to go through," said Jack, pointing toward a double-doored archway.

The three quickly made their way across the entrance hall and entered the meeting room. Jack flipped a clunky switch, and a large set of lights mounted to iron beams in the middle of the room popped on, illuminating the dark, dusty space.

The room was square with no windows, and the brightly colored tapestries of impressive battle scenes that hung on the walls were showing signs of age. A round wooden table surrounded by twelve chairs sat in the middle of the space and was topped with a three-dimensional map of the kingdom as it existed back in medieval times, when the knights were called upon to build prosperity and protect the people.

"Look at this!" Albert exclaimed, running his hand across the contours of the mountains and valleys all carefully carved into the map. "The knights would have used this for planning battles and movements around their kingdom."

"Yeah, that really is pretty cool. They probably had little models of men and knights and horses," replied Jack.

"But where's the clue? Alice did say it would be harder to find this one," said Emma as she wandered around the room, studying the tapestries.

"Why wouldn't she just tell us?" Jack groaned as he began hunting for the clue.

"I think she wanted us to work for it, to earn it," Albert replied as he joined the search.

"Fine, no problem. We can do this," said Jack, feeling more determined.

The three spent quite some time searching, inspecting the table, the chairs, the floor, and the ceiling until Emma let out an excited shriek.

"I've found something!"

"What is it, Em?" Jack rushed to where she was holding one of the tapestries away from the wall.

"There's a word behind here, it's just one word, *strong*. Let's check behind the others,

start over there. It probably goes left to right," said Emma, pointing to the tapestry nearest the doorway.

Jack, Emma, and Albert wasted no time in going from one banner to the next, and Albert wrote down each word as they went.

"*The keys you need are strong indeed, forged of steel, they spin the wheel.*" Albert recited the passage.

"Hey, look over here," Jack called out, "the ground is different under these drawers."

Beneath a set of oak drawers with carved lion claw legs, Jack noticed some wooden planks that were a lighter color and had been cut differently from the rest of the flooring.

"Well, this could be something," Albert said as he bent down and shone his flashlight under the furniture.

"I need some help to move the drawers," said Jack as he stood at one end and strained to lift the heavy old chest.

Emma and Albert quickly arranged themselves around the cabinet. Together, with some effort and grunting, they managed to shift the heavy object far enough away from the wall to reveal the whole section.

"Look, there's a cut-out big enough to fit a hand in," Emma squealed.

"I see it! Looks like a trapdoor or something. Maybe a secret entrance to where the sword is hidden?" Jack was excited as he crouched down to grab hold of the wooden trapdoor.

Jack lifted the door above the stone floor. Emma and Albert wriggled their arms underneath to help pull it open.

"Oh wow, it *is* a secret passage, and in the knight's special meeting room, too!" Emma's eyes twinkled.

The three flashlight beams shone down into the hole, illuminating a ladder and several cobwebs stretching across the passageway.

"Looks like no one's been down here in a while," noted Albert.

"It definitely leads somewhere, though," Jack replied.

"Maybe it is the deep underground clue after all?" Albert pondered.

"But it doesn't look like it goes round and round. Down and underground, yes, but not around," Emma observed.

"That's true, but right now we don't have any other ideas. I'll go first and let you know if it's safe to follow." Jack stepped toward the ladder. "Can you two please shine your lights down so I can see where I'm going?"

Jack tentatively placed a foot at the top of the ladder, and when he felt satisfied that it wasn't about to break under his weight, he began to climb down.

"Alright, I'm near the bottom," Jack called out.

"What do you see? What's down there?" Emma replied.

"Hold on, I'm just turning my flashlight on..." Jack responded as he clicked it on and began waving the bright beam around the dark area. "I don't see any swords or treasure. Actually, it looks a lot like the basement. You two can probably come down if you want to."

Emma and Albert climbed down the ladder to join him.

"I think—" Jack was cut off by a loud creaking sound, followed by a screech. Light began flooding into the darkened area.

"What's that?" Emma asked, her voice a whisper.

"I'm not sure. Hello, is anyone there?" Jack called as he took a few tentative steps toward the light.

"'Allo, who's that?" A gruff voice echoed off the walls and a darkened figure silhouetted against the bright opening was visible ahead of them.

"Wilbur, is that you?" Jack gulped.

"Oh, it's you kids," Wilbur replied.

The loud click of an old light switch sounded as several lights above them buzzed to life and the familiar basement they'd explored earlier suddenly came into view.

"This is just the basement. We were here before," Emma sounded disappointed.

"Oh, I see you kids found the secret passageway in the knight's meeting room then. Well done," Wilbur said with a nod.

"We kind of thought it might lead to the sword," said Albert, looking back up to where they'd come from.

"Good theory, but no, I reckon that was some sort of escape hatch, probably built in case the knights were ever ambushed during a gathering, or the castle came under siege and they couldn't escape through the main door. From down here, they could get to any part of the castle, or outside if need be," Wilbur explained.

"I guess that makes sense. But that doesn't really help us get any closer to this secret room—or the sword," Jack sighed.

"Well, it might not have led where you hoped, but at the very least you've found one more place the sword *isn't* hidden," Wilbur offered.

"True, I suppose that's helpful. We've just got to keep looking, don't we?" Jack grinned.

Wilbur winked. "Well, I can say fairly certainly that it ain't here... I'd quite like to know if there's any truth in this whole legend myself. For whatever it's worth, I'm hoping you succeed. How many of those passages or clues have you got now? Did you find the one up there, behind the tapestries?"

Albert flicked through the pages of his notebook. "The one about the strong keys? We found it and I've written it down. We have four clues now: the entrance hall, the fountain, the ballroom, and the knight's cabinet."

"And we checked out the library and had a look around here in the basement and the dungeon too, but we haven't found anything yet," added Jack.

"Those are the four I know of, and I've followed the same trails you have... there could be more clues hidden, or perhaps there are no more at all. They also might not have anything to do with the sword, just some kind of decoration. It's possible there's no sword to find, or maybe it was found and taken some other place long ago," said Wilbur.

"Yup, those are all possibilities, but I don't think we're ready to give up just yet," said Jack. "There are still lots of places to look and we've got the rest of the afternoon and another day tomorrow to search."

The daylight streaming into the basement from the opening where Wilbur had entered had taken on the orange hue of late afternoon. Jack took a deep breath and filled his thoughts with positivity. They were still no closer to finding the sword, and now time was ticking away. But there was no way Jack was ready to give up.

"Hey guys, why don't we take a look around outside, see if there's anything we've missed out there?"

"Good plan," Albert replied.

"Sure, it beats this stuffy old basement," Emma giggled.

Wilbur chuckled. "Good luck to you, I admire your determination."

After returning the furniture back in place in the knight's cabinet, Jack, Emma, and Albert made their way out the main entrance of the castle and began looking around the outside walls.

The crisp air felt cooler as the sun dipped low on the horizon, and the smell of the salty sea gave the afternoon a sprinkle of magic, as though anything was possible.

The castle was so enormous that it took them almost an hour to walk all the way around the base of it. They discovered interesting architecture, more dragon statues and other sculptures, but no more clues. The last place they visited was the main lookout, which stood several stories higher than the castle itself.

The tower provided an incredible view in every direction, out to sea, over the woods, and along the coast. It was even possible to make out the nearby village.

"It's incredible up here!" said Emma as she gazed out toward the ocean, the sky awash with purple and orange. "Alice was so lucky to grow up in a place like this. So many areas to explore."

"Yeah, it's so amazing!" Albert agreed. "I think sword or no sword, I'd like to come back here again."

"It is pretty cool," Jack replied. "Hey, look, that's our car!" Jack pointed toward the driveway. "Let's go and say hi!"

That evening, Jack, Emma, and Albert filled everyone in on their day around the castle. Alice and Oscar were impressed they had found all the known clues and encouraged them to keep up their search, even though there might not be anything to find at all.

CHAPTER EIGHT

"Guys, you've got to wake up!"

Jack grumbled as his friend startled him.

"Wake up! I think I've got an idea," Albert's voice persisted.

"Go back to sleep, it's too early," Emma groaned sleepily and rolled over.

"What's going on?" asked Jack as he sat up and stretched, yawning as his eyes adjusted to the pale morning light.

Jack saw Albert seated at the desk on the far side of the room, buried in his notebook.

"I woke up with an idea about the clues," Albert replied.

"Yeah, okay, like you know where the sword is?" Jack pushed back the covers and jumped from his bunk to join Albert.

"Well, not quite, but maybe it gets us a *little* closer to it," said Albert, pointing to his notes.

Jack looked down and frowned. "That's just the clues written out again?"

"I know, but what if it isn't just one clue that's the right one, what if it's all of them put together?"

Jack's face lit up with promise as he looked again.

"I've been up for a bit trying different ways to arrange them; putting the clues in this order seems to make the most sense."

Jack read Albert's notes.

Where trees once proud hold knowledge bound, follow what is written to secrets hidden.

The keys you need are strong indeed, forged of steel they spin the wheel.

As the world turns toward the east, look yonder to our winged beast.

Round and round, deep underground, leads the way to secrets found.

"Wow, okay, I kind of see it... nice work, Albert! So, we start in the library and find some strong keys. I wonder what the 'world turning' and 'winged beast' parts mean, though."

Albert removed his glasses and began cleaning them. "Remember that globe in the library? Well, combined with the first clue, I think it might have something to do with that—"

"And maybe there's something on the globe that leads the way?" Jack blurted, his excitement getting the better of him as the pieces started clicking together in his mind.

"Maybe, I'm still not sure either, but I definitely think the library holds the *key*, get it?" Albert chuckled and winked at Jack.

"You two are making so much noise, how am I supposed to sleep?" Emma grumbled as she sat up in her bunk and rubbed her eyes. "It does sound kind of intriguing though; I think we should go investigate Albert's theory."

Jack, Emma, and Albert dressed quickly and grabbed their flashlights before racing excitedly through the hallway, down the stairs, across the entrance hall, and into the library. It was a new day, and they were eager to find out if Albert's discovery had moved them one step closer to solving the mystery.

"So, clue one points to the library. Now we need to figure out what clues two and three could mean," said Jack, as his eyes darted around the area before settling on the ancient globe in the middle of the room. "Do you suppose we could turn that?"

"Let's try," said Albert.

Jack pressed his hands against the metal. It felt cool and smooth as he tried to push and pull it, but it wouldn't budge.

Albert leaned in closer and turned on his flashlight, pointing the beam toward the area where the bronze globe was attached to the stone podium.

"I don't think this part turns. The metal is bolted into the stone," Albert began as he shifted his attention lower. "There's a seam here, between the two pieces of stone, where the top sits on the stand part below. It's possible this might be able to move. Help me push—here, maybe we can use these slots on the sides as handles."

Albert placed one hand on the side of the stone and pushed his fingers into one of the slots. Jack and Emma did the same on the other side.

"1... 2... 3... push," Jack counted to help coordinate everyone's movement.

The top of the stone shifted the smallest amount, but then settled back again.

"Whoa, I think it moved. Did you feel that?"

"Yeah, just a little," Emma agreed with an enthusiastic nod.

"I definitely felt it," replied Albert, moving around to look more closely at the stone.

"Let's try again. Push as hard as we can," said Jack.

Once more, the three took their positions around the stone podium and pushed. Again the stone seemed to shift slightly, then stopped. No matter how much they shoved and strained, it wouldn't move any further.

"Okay, stop pushing," said Albert stepping back and tilting his head to one side, seeming to study the globe and its stand. "It feels like it can move, but something is stopping it. I think if we are going to get this turning it's going to take our brains more than our muscles."

"No problem, we've got both," Jack winked. "We need to figure out where these keys are. The clue talks about *'strong keys'*".

"I agree, and we also need to work out where they would go," said Albert as he crouched down beside the podium and shone his flashlight into one of the slots.

Albert studied the three identical holes, shining his flashlight into each.

"Can you see anything in there?" asked Jack.

"Yeah, there's something. Looks like metal, but it's deep, all the way in the middle."

"Could it be the sword?" Emma asked.

Albert shook his head. "I don't think so, it's more like some sort of metal at the end of it.

It might be something important or it might just be part of how the globe attaches to the stone. Unless we take it apart, it would be tough to know for sure."

"It just feels like we're close here. We've looked all over the castle, and if you're right about the clues being put together, then this seems like the right room... we've got a 'world' that seems like it might be able to turn, the winged beast could be the big dragon on the wall over there. We just need to find the keys..." Jack held his chin and paced back and forth as he thought through the situation.

"There aren't really any keyholes here either, just these slots, but I've never seen a key that big or that shape before," Albert sighed, looking over the globe and podium again.

The daylight streaming in through the windows was getting brighter as the sun continued to rise, and a glint of reflected sunlight caught Emma's eye, drawing her attention toward one of the walls.

"The swords!" Emma cried, racing toward them.

"What?" asked Jack, looking confused.

"Think about it, Jack, they're made of steel, they're 'strong indeed', and they would probably fit into those slots," Emma replied as she reached them.

Albert looked from the swords to the podium and back again, slowly nodding his head. "You make a good point, Emma, and three swords as well as three slots here. It's worth a try, let's see if we can get one down."

It took a few minutes of fiddling, but they were soon able to open the old latch that held the first sword to the wall, possibly the first time it had been opened in hundreds of years.

"Whoa, this is heavier than I expected. Wow, those knights must have been super strong,"

Jack remarked as the weight of the sword forced it toward the ground, making a clanking sound.

"Be careful with that thing, Jack," Emma cautioned.

"Yeah, this is some seriously heavy metal!" laughed Jack as he gripped the sword more confidently and made his way to the podium.

Jack held the end of the sword up near the slot in the podium. "It looks like it will fit perfectly."

"Well, don't keep us waiting," Albert prompted.

"Okay, here goes." Jack pushed the sword into the slot. There was a scraping sound from within the podium, followed by a metallic *clink* and finally a loud *click*.

The three children gasped.

"Quick, let's get the other two!" Emma squealed, frantically clapping her hands.

They carefully retrieved the remaining swords from the wall and slotted them into the podium, each producing an audible *click* as they locked into place.

"Something has definitely happened in there. Ready to see if these are the keys that free the wheel, like the clue says?" asked Albert.

The swords were mostly inside the podium with the handles sticking out the sides, and Jack, Emma, and Albert each grabbed hold of one.

Jack pointed, "This is the direction we'd need to push to turn the globe toward the east."

Emma and Albert nodded.

"Alright, let's go, 3... 2... 1... *push*," called Jack.

A scraping sound of stone rubbing against stone erupted as the top wheel of the podium—and the globe attached to it— began to turn.

"It's working!" Albert exclaimed.

On the far side of the room, the sound of gears turning and metal groaning drew their attention.

"Guys, look! Something's happening to the dragon!" Emma cried.

CHAPTER NINE

"Keep pushing!" Jack encouraged.

As they continued to push the stone circle, the enormous metal dragon sculpture began to pull away from the wall. Attached to one of two large doors it had concealed, the doors swung open to reveal a darkened room beyond.

"There's a secret room, or a hidden passage, or something back there," Emma shrieked with delight.

"You're right! Just a little more and we'll be able to fit through the gap," Jack replied.

They pushed for another few revolutions until the opening grew wider. Jack, Emma, and Albert grabbed their flashlights and shone them into the darkness.

The faded smell of cedarwood mixed with musty air wafted out from inside the hidden room, as though it had been preserved for centuries.

"Look, a staircase!" Emma exclaimed, directing her flashlight toward the floor.

"A *spiral* staircase," added Jack.

"Round and round, deep underground. It matches the clues!" Albert exclaimed.

"Awesome, let's go!" Jack pointed his flashlight toward the stone staircase and began winding his way downward.

Emma and Albert followed closely behind as they wound their way down, clearing cobwebs and leaving footprints in the deep layer of dust covering the stairs.

"Anyone else feel dizzy?" asked Jack when they reached the bottom.

"Ha-ha!" Albert replied, "Feels like we turned around a dozen times."

"Wow, we're probably the first people down here in like hundreds of years," Jack scanned the area with his flashlight.

"There's another door," said Albert.

Jack and Emma followed Albert's light to a metal door with square stud patterns and iron pins in the framework.

"And some sort of table here, too," said Jack as his flashlight beamed across a rectangular table in the middle of the room. He briefly examined the stone table on his way toward the door.

"There's no handle or lock," said Jack as he pushed against it. "It just won't budge."

"Hmmm, maybe we're missing a clue?" Albert shrugged.

"This table might have something to do with opening the door," said Emma. "Actually, it seems more like a whole lot of buttons or something, like an ancient kind of control panel." She took a closer look with her flashlight and pressed one of the buttons. It sank down with a *click*.

"Wait, what if pushing the buttons does something?" said Albert as he joined Emma at the table.

"Well, I'm sure they do *something*. Why else would this be here?" Emma replied, and pushed another button.

This time the button, along with the first one she'd pushed, rose back up to their original positions again.

"I mean, what if something bad happens?" huffed Albert, "Like opening a trap-door that drops us into a pit of sharp spikes or snakes or I don't know, something *bad*."

"Whoa man, what's all this talk about snakes?" said Jack. "Let's not push anything until we're sure it's safe." His attention and flashlight shifted to the ground beneath them.

"Or, what if it's the way to open the door?" Emma countered.

"Well, sure, it could be. I'm just saying we should be careful," Albert replied as he touched several of the buttons on the table but didn't press them down.

"Seems like the floor is all made of stone, so hopefully there aren't any trapdoors," Jack sounded relieved.

"There's some writing at the edges here, etched into the stone," said Albert, using his hand to wipe away a thick layer of dust. *"Across the sky, taking flight by night, his course is clear as our cause is true."*

"Another clue! Maybe it's how we open the door." Jack put his hand on his chin, thinking about what the riddle might mean.

"Dragons, Draco—there are so many references about dragons around here... and all the dragons have wings, they fly," Emma offered as the three stood around the table.

"Could be, but how are we supposed to press Draco, there aren't any letters on these buttons... they're shaped more like stars," Albert replied.

"Stars? Wait, that's it... you might both be right!" Jack exclaimed.

"What do you think, Jack?" Albert asked.

"Remember in the entrance hall on the crest, how the stars formed the constellation Draco? Do you get it... *across the sky, taking flight by night*—the buttons are stars. Maybe we just need to push the right ones?"

"Jack, that could totally work!" cried Emma.

"I drew a picture of the constellation! Just a minute." Albert pulled his notebook out of his back pocket, tucked his flashlight under his chin, and flipped through the pages until he found it. Then he held it beside the buttons on the table. "So, do you suppose we just press in the star buttons that match with the constellation?"

"It's a good place to start," Jack replied. "Do you want to do the honors, Em?"

"Of course, I'd love to!" Emma looked back and forward between the buttons and Albert's notebook a few times before reaching out and placing her hand on the first one. "Here goes..."

Emma pushed until it stopped with a *click*.

"Now this one..." Emma pushed the next button down until it clicked as well. "Look, they are both staying down this time. I think we've got this!"

"Yeah, and we haven't fallen through any trapdoors, so that's a good thing... at least not *yet*." Albert raised a single eyebrow and grinned.

Jack looked down toward the hard stone floor once more and shone his flashlight around warily. "So far, so good. Keep going!"

It didn't take long for Emma to press in the rest of the buttons to complete the Draco constellation. Upon pushing the final one, the click was followed by a mechanical rumble coming from the door.

Everyone gasped as they directed their beams of light toward the sound and looked on eagerly as the old door groaned and creaked inward.

"We're so close, I can feel it. Come on, let's go inside," Jack said as he headed for the doorway. Jack shone his flashlight into the dark room and stepped in, followed by Emma and Albert.

"It's... amazing!" Jack exclaimed. "We've found it. That must be the sword—check out the dragon detail engraved into the handle!"

"Wow! Look at all this stuff. Old scrolls, chests, armor—wait until we tell everyone about this!" added Albert.

The children knew they had uncovered a very special piece of Alice's family history, as well as some ancient and valuable treasures.

Jack picked up the sword, Emma grabbed an armful of scrolls, and Albert collected a knight's helmet as well as an old flag which bore the Order of the Dragon's crest. They carefully carried them back up the spiral staircase and into the library.

With a plan to surprise their hosts, the children asked Wilbur for help. They spent the afternoon setting up some of the most special items, including placing the sword into the display cabinet.

That evening, Jack, Emma, and Albert could hardly contain their excitement when they asked Alice and Oscar to meet them in the entrance hall after dinner. When they noticed the sword resting proudly in the display cabinet, Alice yelled in shock. Once the disbelief had passed, she expressed how thrilled she was that such an enduring mystery had now been solved. She promised to set up displays for all the other treasures the children had found in the secret room and thanked them for their persistence and resourcefulness which led to the discovery.

"Well, you children have most certainly made this a *'knight'* to remember!" said Mr. Jones.

Everyone laughed.

THE END

JACK JONES

TITLES IN THIS SERIES

www.jackjonesclub.com

ABOUT THE AUTHOR

Zander Bingham was born and raised on a boat. It was captured by pirates when he was just 12 years old. He, along with his family and crew, swam to a nearby island where Zander spent his days imagining swashbuckling adventures on the high seas.

Well, not exactly.

But Zander did love boating adventures as a kid. And he always dreamed of exploring deserted islands and being a real-life castaway. He grew up cruising around Australia, the USA and The Bahamas. He eventually captained his very own sailboat, living aboard and exploring the Adriatic Sea with his wife and two young sons.

His thirst for exploration, his witty sense of humor, and his new-found passion for writing stories to read to his boys at bedtime, led to the creation of Jack Jones; the confident, brave and curious boy adventurer who is always searching for his next escapade.

Made in the USA
Las Vegas, NV
13 September 2024

95213471R00062